Paul

MYTHICAL IRISH BEASTS

First published in 2018 by Currach Press
23 Merrion Square
Dublin 2
Ireland
www.currach.ie

ISBN: 978-1-78218-905-3

Set in Gill Sans 9/15 and Peach Milk
Book design by Alba Esteban | Currach Press
Front and back cover by Mark Joyce
Printed by Jellyfish Solutions

CURRACH
P R E S S

MYTHICAL IRISH BEASTS

MARK JOYCE

CURRACH PRESS

For my parents, Kevin and Margriet Joyce

Who taught me to dream with my eyes open, so I could see my dreams come true.

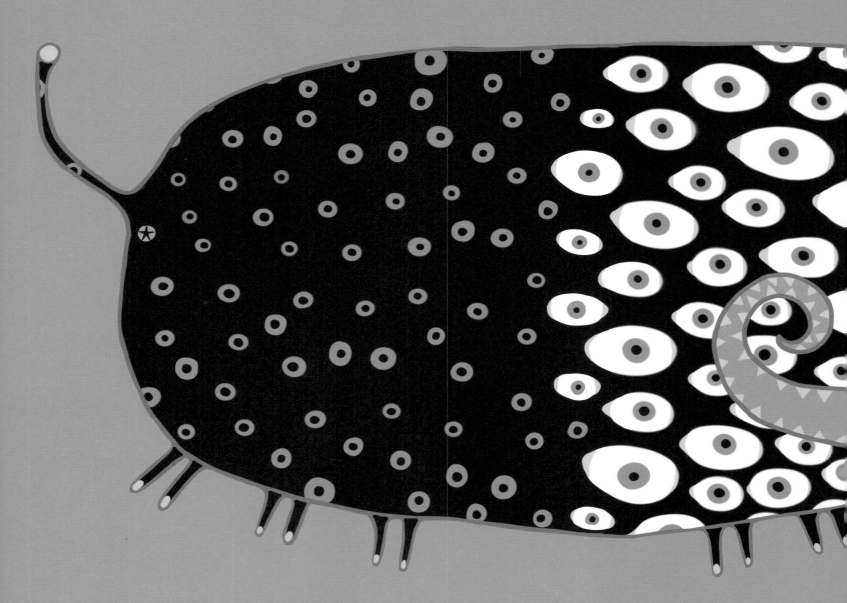

PREFACE

There is a magic in Ireland that is at first hard to grasp; like most things of quality, it takes time to fully appreciate it. On the surface its beauty is obvious, the little lakes full of salmon and trout scattered like sapphires and diamonds across the landscape. The hidden valleys and mysterious glens, quiet peninsulas and out-of-the-way inlets are captivating. The way the rivers flow from the mountains, winding their way across the landscape to the sea. But this is only the surface view of an old land that is full of mystery and magic.

When St Patrick came to Ireland as a young slave from Wales, he arrived to an ancient pagan landscape full of the legends of cattle raids and fantastic stories of heroes and their feats of courage and strength. Popular as well were myths surrounding sea serpents, or 'ullpheists', and magic cows with unending supplies of milk. Thankfully many of these old legends were recorded in early medieval manuscripts like the Acallam na Senórach, which translates as 'Tales of the Elders', which dates back to the 12th century and is the longest surviving work of original medieval Irish literature.

In Ireland we are also lucky to have treasure books full of ancient folklore and tales written by such illustrious people as William Wilde (Oscar's father), and W. B. Yeats, to name just a few. These writers follow in the tradition of Acallam na Senorach, telling of Irish monsters that crawl in the deep, giants and beasts, and quirky creatures like the immortal Crane of Iniskea Island or the white trout of Cong.

They were adding to ancient stories from the book of Ballymote, and others dating back to the Middle Ages. These medieval books contain the familiar Irish stories of 'Cuchulain', 'The Children of Lir' and 'Tír na nÓg'.

But if you continue reading you will find tales of Glarcus the Giant and the Suilleach, that many eyed monster in Donegal that is the source of the river Swilly.

I have long been fascinated with the legends and folklore of Ireland. As a child my parents would often bring me to places associated with these stories. Máméan is one such place, situated in the mountains near my home. Máméan is a pilgrimage site now associated with St Patrick. However, if you delve a little further into the story of Máméan, you will find a more ancient tale of the half man, half bull 'Crom Dubh' and of the epic battle between Ireland's pagan past and the new Roman religion of St Patrick. On the mountain pass of Máméan, St Patrick fought the pagan god Crom Dubh. St Patrick won the battle, and after he killed Crom Dubh he threw him into a small lake in the mountain pass that is now named Loch an Tairbh, or 'lake of the bull'. There is a further macabre part of this story: since that day, the lake has had a red hue resulting from the blood of Crom Dubh.

I hope this book will be a happy introduction to many of the lesser-known magical creatures and beasts of Ireland, as well as a few familiar ones. *Mythical Irish Beasts* is based in part on a medieval bestiary (though these books often had a moral story attached, which I will forgo). Sadly, I cannot include every mystic Irish creature, though that would be a worthy project.

The inspiration for this little book comes from many places, including Jorge Luis Borges' *The Book of Imaginary Beings*, but also P.W. Joyce's book, *The Wonders of Ireland* is a favourite, and some of the creatures from his book have been included in this one. Unlike Borges, I have decided to include some of the legends concerning human transformation, because here we see early legends like the werewolf coming into existence. Surely one of the earliest mentions of werewolves in the world must be the tale 'The Man Wolves of Ossary' based on the 12th century book, *The History and Topography of Ireland* by Gerard of Wales.

My sources for this book are numerous, including the aforementioned Gerard of Wales, a number of wonderful medieval Irish manuscripts and Thomas Crofton Croker's book, *Fairy Legends and Traditions of the South of Ireland*. Materials from the Ossianic Society have also been a treasure. From these and other works I have at all times worked from translation and often paraphrased when taking a direct quote, but always acknowledge the original source.

The nature of this book demands that many of the legends associated with these creatures be summarised. Some, like the Glas Goibheann or 'cow of plenty' have many legends from around Ireland associated with them and have had to be massively condensed.

I have included a portion of the epic poem 'The Fenian hunt of Sliabh Truim', translated by the Ossianic Society in 1854 not only because of the numerous creatures it mentions, but also because surely Ard-na-g-cat must be the most impressive monster in Irish legend that nobody knows about.

In Ireland I believe we are still close to this realm of 'other'. It is in our national DNA. Fairy rings are left intact and hawthorn trees are left uncut for fear of fairy retribution. This other realm is also still in our native place-names, like Bru Si or 'fairyhouse' in Co. Meath, Abberanville or 'great beast' in Co. Galway, and Pollpeasty or 'pool of the monstrous reptile' in Wexford.

Regarding the illustrations of these mythical Irish beasts, I have tried to give them a more contemporary feel, while acknowledging that no image can compete with a dark room and a malevolent scratching at the door.

Mark Joyce

CONTENTS

AONBÁRR

 onbárr of the Flowing Mane was the name of a magical horse belonging to Manannán mac Lir, Ireland's sea god.

This horse could traverse both land and sea. In Irish mythology, Manannán travelled over the waves, most often in a chariot but sometimes on horseback.

The meaning of this name can be explained as 'One Mane' with aon meaning 'one' and bárr meaning 'hair', 'tip', or 'horse's mane'.

Another horse with similar powers comes from the legendary story of Oisin and Niamh in Tír na nÓg, 'Land of Youth'. Oisín falls in love with the Princess Niamh, from the Land of Youth, and she invites him to travel with her over the sea on a magical horse.

'There was a wide, long, smooth garment
Covering the white [steed] horse;
A carved saddle of red gold,
And she had a bridle with a mouth bit of gold in her right hand.
There were four shapely shoes under him
Of the yellow gold of most clear brightness,
A wreath of silver at the back of his head,
And there was not in the world a steed which was better.

Oisin in the Land of Youth,
Micheál Coimín, 1750

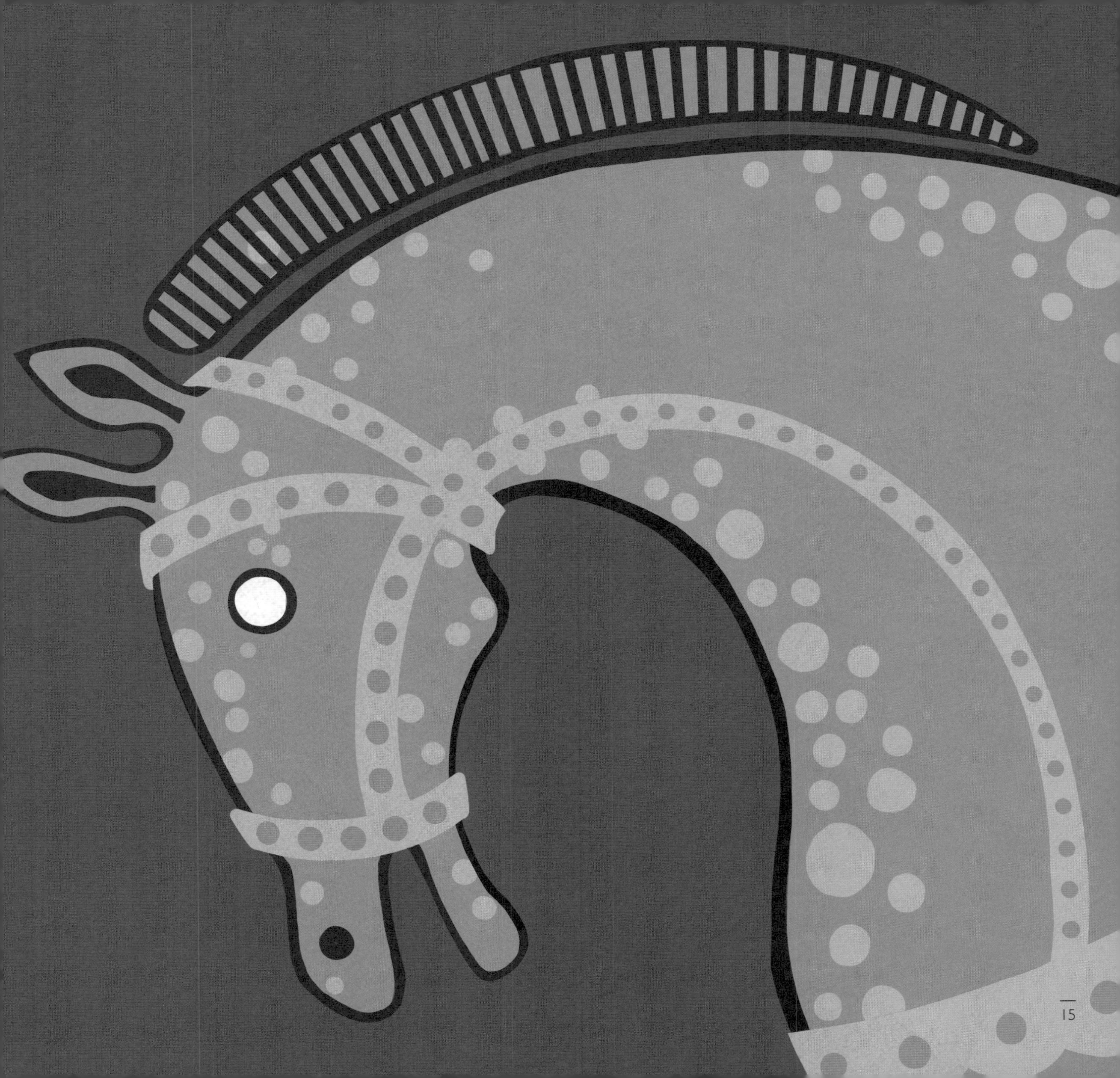

THE MERROW

The Merrow is the Irish name for a mermaid or merman, though another popular term is maighdean-mhara which translates as 'sea maiden'.

The Irish Merrow is human shaped from the waist up, with a fish-like tail from the waist down. She is often seen with a comb like the Banshee.

The Merrow wears a special cap called a 'Cohuleen druith'; this gives her the power to dive and swim in the ocean. According to legend, if a Merrow loses her Cohuleen druith she also loses the ability to swim beneath the waves. Cohuleen druith literally translates as 'little magic hood'.

There are reported sightings of mermaids from all around the coast of Ireland, including mention of a mermaid in the freshwater Lough Owel in Westmeath.

In *The Book of Invasions*[1] there is a story of mermaids playing round the ships of the Milesians, the final race to settle in Ireland.

There is also a variant to the etymology of Port Lairge in Co. Waterford that involves merrows. In the Dindsenchas[2], one story explains how mermaids killed a man named Roth. According to this legend, the mermaids dismembered Roth, leaving only his thigh bone, which washed ashore, and this is how Port Lairge or 'Port of the Thigh' got its name.

1. The Book of Invasions, or 'Lebor Gabála Érenn', is a collection of poems and prose dating back to the 11th century that details the history of Ireland from creation to the Middle Ages.
2. The Dindshenchas translates as 'the lore of places' and from it we get a greater understanding of place names as well as legends and traditions. It is comprised of poems and tales. These date from the 11th to the 15th century.

DOBHAR-CHÚ: 'THE KING OF OTTERS'

The Dobhar-chú is the father of all the otters in Ireland and is considered 'King of the Lakes'.

The meaning of Dobhur-chú could be explained as 'water hound'. The modern Irish word for water is 'uisce', although 'dobhar' is an old and rarely used Irish word that has Celtic references to water. Cú is 'hound' in Irish. It should be noted that dobharchú is also the modern Irish word for 'otter'.

The Dobhar-chú is fearsome, with a snout so powerful it can break through rock. He kills both people and animals and drinks their blood.

There is a headstone, found in Conwall cemetery in Glenade, Co. Leitrim, that depicts the Dobhar-chú. The headstone belongs to Gráinne Ni Conalai. It is claimed that she was killed by the Dobhar-chú in 1772. Her husband supposedly heard her scream as she was washing clothes at Glenade Lough, and came to her aid. When he got there she was already dead, with the Dobhar-chú feasting on her bloody and mutilated body. The man killed the Dobhar-chú, stabbing it in the heart. As it died, it made a whistling noise, and its mate arose from the lough. The man chased the beast, and after a long and bloody battle, it was also killed.

In 1684, Irish historian Roderick O'Flaherty wrote of an encounter with an Irish crocodile, which we can presume to be the Dobhar-Chú. He wrote, "The man was on the shore of Lough Mask when he saw the head of a beast swimming in the water. He thought it was an otter. The creature seemed to look at him, it then swam underwater where it reached land, it grabbed the man by his elbow and dragged him into the lake, the man took his knife from his pocket and stabbed it, which scared the animal away."

SUILEACH

he River Swilly in Donegal gets its name from a multi-eyed monster that lived in a pool, which is the source of the river at Meenaroy. The monster had two hundred eyes on either side of its head and hence was called Suileach, or 'full of eyes', from the Irish word for eye, 'suil'.

St Columba or Columcille (521–597), who was from Donegal, was thought to have chased the creature back to his lair at the source of the river. There was a great fight, and the saint cut the monster in two with his sword. The creature's tail wrapped itself around Columcille's body and started to squeeze while its head crept forward with its toothy mouth, ready to bite. Just when all hope seemed lost, Columcille freed himself and pierced the monster's head, killing it. Columcille is also connected to a sighting of the Loch Ness monster which appears later in this book.

THE MAN WOLVES OF OSSORY

In the 12th century, Gerald of Wales wrote a history and topography of Ireland. This book was an account of his journeys around Ireland, the landscapes, the flora and fauna as well as fantastic stories of strange creatures and malevolent beasts. This is one legend set in Ossory, in Co. Kilkenny.

A priest was travelling in the countryside when two wolves approached him and began to speak. One wolf said "Do not fear me" and went on to explain that both he and his fellow wolf had been cursed by the abbot Natalis, and that the curse compelled both the man and woman to be exiled, not only from their own land but also from their bodies, and so they took the form of wolves. The wolf also explained that if he and his companion survived as wolves for seven years, two others would have to take their place.

The wolf now beseeched the priest to give his companion solace, as she was gravely ill. The priest duly granted her the Christian last rites.

An account of this story was documented by the bishop and abbots of the time at a synod. These documents as well as the priest's confession were sealed with the seals of the bishops and abbots present and sent to the Pope in Rome.

There is a follow-up to this story recorded for the 'Irish Archaeological Society' by John O'Donovan in 1842 that says, "The descendants of the wolf are in Ossory. They have a wonderful property. They can transform themselves into wolves and go forth in the form of wolves, and if they happen to be killed with flesh in their mouths, it is in the same condition that the bodies out of which they have come are found; and they command their families not to remove their bodies, because if they were moved they could never come into them again."

MUIRDRIS OR SINACH

 ergus mac Léti was the King of Ulster. Once, when he was sleeping by water, he was captured by water-sprites called Lúchorpáin or 'little bodies' (interestingly this is thought to be the first reference to leprechauns). These little creatures tried to drag Fergus into the sea while he was asleep, but the cold water woke him and he seized them.

In exchange for their freedom, the Lúchorpáin granted him three wishes, one of which was to gain the ability to breathe underwater. However, there was a stipulation that Fergus would not be allowed to use this gift in Loch Rudraige, 'Dundrum Bay', his own homeland. Despite the warning, he attempted to dive there anyway. While in the bay he encountered a sea-monster called Muirdris. When Fergus looked at the beast, his face contorted in terror.

This disfigurement should have disqualified him from his kingship, but the Ulstermen did not want to depose him, so they banned mirrors from his presence so he would never learn of his deformity.

Seven years later, when he was whipping a serving girl, in anger she revealed the truth of his disfigurement to him. Fergus returned to Loch Rudraige in search of the sea-monster, and after a two-day battle he killed it, before he himself died of exhaustion. For a whole month afterward, the lake remained red with the blood of the monster.

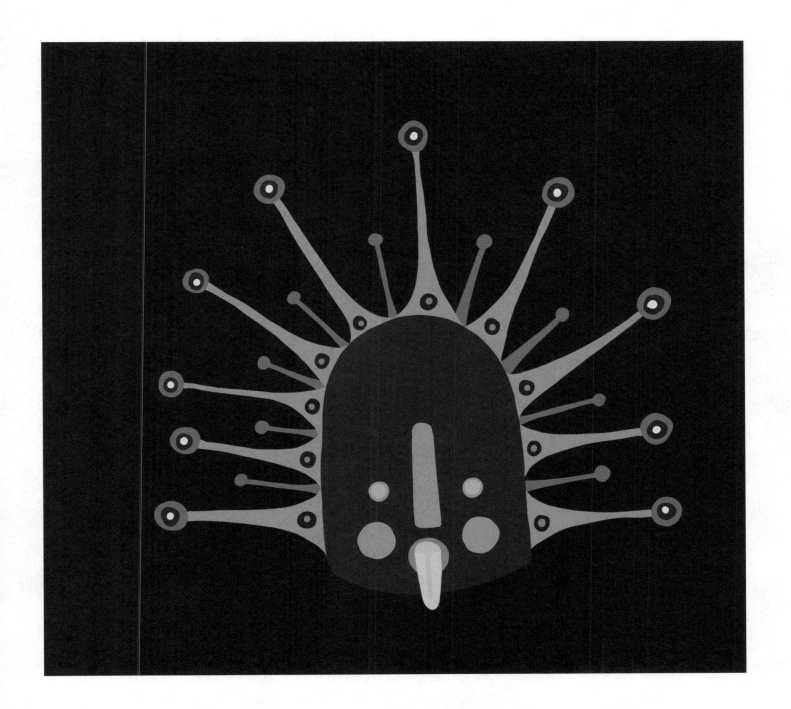

CLOBHAIR-CEANN, CLURICHAUN

he Clobhair-Ceann is one of Ireland's solitary faerys[1]; others include the Fear Dearg and the famous Leprechaun.

Nicholas O'Kearney, a famous 19th century folklorist, described the Clobhair-Ceann as "a jolly, red-faced, drunken little fellow, and was ever found in the cellars of the rich, Bachus-like, astride the wine barrel with a brimful tankard in hand, drinking and singing away merrily. Any wine cellar known to be haunted by this sprite, was doomed to bring its owner to speedy ruin." [2]

There is a further account by James Graves writing about the Clobhair-Ceann and his association with Carrick Castle, or Ormonde Castle, in Co. Tipperary. This particular fairy had the name "Leather Apron" and his job was to see that the serving men and women of the castle did their duty on threat of a thrashing from the leather apron that gave him his name.

The Clobhair-Ceann always carries a purse with him which is called the 'spre-na-skillinagh', and it is said he is never without a shilling in it.

For fun he was known to harness a sheep or shepherd's dog and ride them purely for his own amusement.

The Clubhair-Ceann belongs to the cordwainer[3] class of Irish faerys.

1. The Irish poet W. B. Yeats divided Irish faerys into two classes; 'trooping faerys' who often appeared in groups or parties and 'solitary faerys' who appeared on their own. The folklorist Katherine Mary Briggs noted that a possible third class of 'domesticated faerys' could be added.

2. Feis Tithe Chonáin, 1855.

3. A 'cordwainer' is a shoemaker who makes shoes from new leather as opposed to a cobbler, who is restricted to repairing shoes.

ENCHANTMENTS

This little book tells the tale of a number of humans who have been changed into animals, and the following is another such story.

The King of Dreoluinn's daughter had a violent hatred for Faithleann Mongshuileach, daughter of the king's former wife. She brought the girl to bathe in Eas Beobhuinne, a water-hole close to the king's palace, and there she was enchanted. The following were the bonds under which she enchanted her: to remain one year a cat, another a swan, and the third a venomous otter, but she could assume her own shape one day in each year.[1]

It should be noted that possibly the most unusual enchantment was a Fenian man who became a female every alternate year.

1. Transactions of the Ossianic Society, Vol 2, 1854.

DEALRA DUBH

Fionn MacCumhaill is the ultimate Irish hero and his quests are legendary. Fionn always appears on foot and does not have a favoured horse or a chariot like the other Irish hero, Cúchulainn.

Fionn has battles with many exotic entities, but the most ominous is Dealra Dubh or dark sheen. This malignant opponent could be described as an evil-minded cloud of death. Whosoever met him while fasting in the morning would be certain of meeting with nothing but ill luck the rest of that day. Another demon of the air is the Deamhan Aeir, who taunts the children of Lir. According to P.W. .Joyce, the 'Bocanachs' (male goblins) and 'Bananachs' (females) were often in the company of the 'Deamhan Aeir'.

LIATH MACHA AND DUBH SAINGLEND 'BLACK SHANGLAN': THE MAGIC HORSES OF CÚCHULAINN

iath Macha or 'grey of Macha' and Dub Sainglend 'Black of Shanglan' are the two chariot-horses of the Irish hero Cúchulainn.

Liath Macha came from Emain Macha (Navan Fort) and magically rose from a lake before being tamed by Cúchulainn.

"Ireland quaked from the centre to the sea. They reeled together, steed and hero, through the plains of Murthemney. 'Make the circuit of Ireland Liath Macha and I shall be on the neck of thee,' cried Cúchulainn. The horse went in reeling circles round Ireland. Cúchulainn mightily thrust the bit into his mouth and made fast the headstall. The Liath Macha went a second time round Ireland. The sea retreated from the shore and stood in heaps. Cúchulainn sprang upon his back. A third time the horse went round Ireland, bounding from peak to peak. They seemed a resplendent Fomorian phantom against the stars. The horse came to a stand. 'I think thou art tamed, O Liath Macha," said Cúchulainn.'

The Coming of Cuculain by Standish James O'Grady, 1894:

"Black Shanglan came from the dark valley. The Liath Macha was grey to whiteness, the other horse was black and glistening like the bright mail of the chaffer. He rode thence to Emain Macha with the two horses like a lord of Day and Night, and of Life and Death."

AIRETECH AND HIS THREE WEREWOLF DAUGHTERS

In Irish folklore, Airetech was a creature from the Otherworld, the last of an oppressive company. He lived with his three beautiful daughters in Cave Cruachan, today Rathcroghan Complex in Co. Roscommon, which, presumably, had an opening into the otherworld. At will or by their father's bidding, his daughters could shape shift into vicious werewolves. Every year they came and destroyed whatever rams and sheep were owned by Cailte, who was a nephew of Fionn MacCumhail.[1]

Cailte pleaded with the bard to kill them. Cas the Bard said to them, "If you really are human it would be better for you to listen to the music in human shape rather than as wolves." They listened to him, and took off their dark, long cloaks that they had been wearing. They did this easily because of their love for Cas' music. While they were listening to Cas, Cailte sent his poisonous spear,[2] which went "through the nipple of the breast of the woman furthest away, having already gone through the other two women, so that all three were strung together on the spear. Cas Corach went over to them and cut off their heads".[3] And this valley has been known as the Valley of the Wolf Shapes ever since.[4]

1. Fionn MacCumhail is a legendary hero from Irish legend. He is the leader of the tribe 'The Fianna'.
2. The spear had the name 'forefinger of valour'.
3. Catherine E. Karkov, 'Tales of the Ancients', Postcolonial Moves: Medieval Through Modern, p. 104.
4. This valley is to the north of Bricriu's cairn near Rathcroghan Complex in Co. Roscommon.

FISH WITH THREE GOLDEN TEETH

Gerald of Wales was one of the world's first travel writers. He studied in France and visited the Pope in Rome. He had aspirations to become the Bishop of the Diocese of St Davids in Wales, but Gerald was quite prejudiced against the Irish. He portrayed them as barbaric savages.

In 1185 Gerald of Wales wrote an account of his trip to Ireland in a book he called *Topographia Hibernica* or 'The Topography of Ireland'. In it he describes a magical fish with three golden teeth.

'Two years before the coming of the English to the Island, there was at Carlingford¹ in Ulster a fish of unusual size and quality. Among other wonderful things about it was that it had three teeth of gold of about fifty ounces' weight in all. It seemed to prefigure the imminent conquest of the country.''

1. Carlingford is a large sea inlet in Northern Ireland. The name Carlinford translates from the old Norse to 'narrow sea-inlet of the hag'.

ALP-LUACHRA

There are not many descriptions as to their visage, but Robert Kirk in his 1893 book *The Secret Commonwealth of Elves, Fauns & Fairies* explains that Alp-Luachra are "lean like a heron or hawk notwithstanding his devouring appetite". One story tells of the Alp-Luachra or 'joint eater'.[1] The story goes that there was once a wealthy farmer from Connaught, who fell asleep beside a stream, ,and when he woke he had a pain in his belly.

His sickness got worse and worse and he started to lose weight, no matter how much he ate. He spent all his fortune on doctors trying to get a cure for his illness, but to no avail. Eventually when all hope seemed lost he met a beggar man, who concluded that his ailment was as a result of the Alp-Luachra. The only cure was to go to the Prince of Coolavin. The prince instructed him to eat salted beef and then brought him to the brink of the stream, where he told him to lie down on his stomach over the stream, hold his face over the water and open his mouth as wide as he could.

The sick man was lying like that for less than a quarter of an hour when something began moving inside of him, and he felt something coming up in his throat. The prince said in a whisper: "Now the thirst's coming on them; the salt that was in the beef is working them; now they'll come out." "There's a dozen of them now," said the prince. Eventually with much pain the mother of the little beasts came out to join her brood in the water. With this and a good meal, the man was cured.

1. This story is taken from Douglas Hyde's 1890 book *Beside the Fire*.

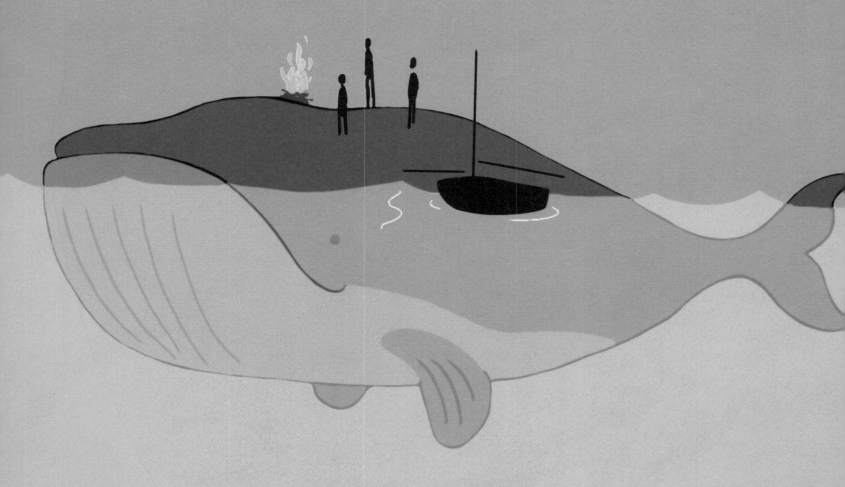

BEAST JASCONIUS

S t Brendan, born in 484 and died in 577, was probably best known for his legendary journey in a leather boat from Ireland across the Atlantic to North America. This voyage, known as 'The Voyage of St Brendan the Navigator', was put into book form around AD 900.

In the book there are 29 chapters, and in one chapter he finds an island of sheep, in another a gryphon and a dragon/bird battle. The battle is heroic, with the gryphon tearing the eyes of the dragon and sparks fly from their clashing teeth.[1] Many a wound is given. The gryphon is large and the dragon wins victory by being quick and throwing the dead gryphon into the sea.

Importantly for us, he also encounters a sea monster, the Beast Jasconius.[2]

Brendan and his fellow voyagers are at sea and as it is Easter, they wish to make camp to celebrate the day. They see an island and climb onto it to make camp. When they light their campfire, the island begins to move. Out of fear of the moving island they race to their ship. Once back on the ship, Brendan explains that the moving island is really the beast Jasconius, who labours unsuccessfully to put his tail into his mouth.

1. The gryphon is a legendary creature with the head, talons, and wings of an eagle and the body of a lion.
2. The name is Irish, from 'iasc', the usual word for fish He is described as the largest creature of the deep and is continually trying to join his head to his tail.

IMMORTAL CRANE

he Crane is mentioned quite a lot in Irish legend and folklore. It is noted that if the crane flies high in the middle of the day, it is a sign that good weather will continue; however, if the crane flies low and frequently stops, then rain may be expected. Often the names of the heron and the crane are used to describe the same bird. The most famous mention of the crane in Irish legend is that of the crane bag of Mannanan Mac Lir. Mannanan Mac Lir's name translates to 'Son of the Sea' and he is the chief god associated with the sea. One of his most important possessions is the 'crane bag' that holds all his precious things, including language. Mannanan acquired the bag after the princess Aoife was transformed into a crane. She subsequently lived with Mac Lir for two hundred years, and on her death he made his bag from her skin.

The Immortal Crane comes from the island of Inishkea off the coast of Co. Mayo, where according to the legend a lonely crane lives without any kin. Since Genesis, he has lived there looking down on the Atlantic waves, and he will survive until the day of judgement. Sometimes it is thought that the crane in question is an enchanted person doing some form of penance.

THE MORRIGAN
PART 1

The Morrigan are three sisters named Bodhbh, Macha and Anand who together are called 'The Morrigan'[1]. The Morrigan is the Great Phantom Queen of Ireland, the goddess of war and fate. She is included in this book because she has the ability to transform into a multitude of different animals, including birds and fish, and also has the ability to transform from a beautiful young girl into a hag. The Morrigan's home in Ireland is Rath-Cruachan in Roscommon. Rath-Cruachan is thought be a kind of entrance to the otherworld and is sometimes known as 'Hell's Gate'.

In the epic poem 'Táin Bó Cúailnge', an invasion is launched by Queen Maeve[2] of Connaught to capture the Ulster bull, Donn Cuailnge.[3] Cúchulainn defends Ulster and in between battles, The Morrigan offers him love and aid in battle, which he rejects. Feeling slighted, she retaliates by appearing as an eel that trips him, but he breaks her ribs. Then she appears as a wolf that creates a stampede of cattle, but he pokes the wolf's eye out. When the Morrigan becomes the red heifer leading the stampede, Cúchulainn breaks her leg. Later she appears to Cúchulainn as an old milk cow with the wounds inflicted by Cúchulainn. When Cúchulainn asks for a drink, she allows him to suckle from three teats, and with each drink he blesses her and with each blessing a wound is healed.

At the end of the epic she appears as a hooded crow and famously lands on Cúchulainn shoulder. It is only when she does this that the armies of Connaught believe he has died.

1. Anand is a variant spelling of 'Anu' and also 'Danu/Danaan', from which we get the 'Tuatha DeDanaan', which means Tribe of the Goddess Danaan.
2. Queen Maeve is a legendary figure in Ireland, and is the ultimate warrior queen. Her name can be interpreted as 'mead woman' or 'she who intoxicates'.
3. Donn Cuailnge is a legendary Irish stud bull. He originally was a man named Friuch and there is an explanation as to his becoming a bull in the story on page 103 of Rucht and Friuch.

THE MORRIGAN
PART 2

Badhbh is one of the three 'Morrigan' sisters who appeared before the battle of Moyrath in 637AD. Badhbh is seen as grey haired, lean and nimble, hovering and hopping about on the points of the spears and shields of the army who were to be victorious. She has also been described as "A big mouthed, swarthy, swift, sooty woman, lame and squinting with her left eye."

In Cormac's glossary,[1] Badb is a malignant couple by the name of Neit and his wife to be, Nemon. They are described as being gods in the battle with pagans, and as being a "malignant, bad and venomous couple".

The Morrigan is also a sort of faery phantom that is associated with war, who appeared as three malignant looking witch-hags with blue beards that came out before the battle of Magh Leana shrieking and calling out for victory for 'Conn the Hundred fighter'.

The Morrigan is also represented in the battle of Moyturra, where she appeared with the Dagda[2] before the fighting and promised to destroy the opposing Fomorian army. This she did by reciting a magical poem and driving the Fomorians into the sea.

1. Cormac's glossary is an early Irish glossary of old Irish words dating to the 9th century. The glossary is ascribed to Cormac mac Cullennáin, King-Bishop of Ulster.
2. The Dagda is a god in Irish mythology, and is portrayed as a father figure with power over the weather, time and the seasons as well as life and death.

THE SERPENT OF LOCH CHRAILI

och Chraili is an enchanted lake in Co. Kerry with a ferocious serpent lurking in its depths. Legend has it that there was a child to be baptised by St Cuan, but St Cuan knew that people would not come to the feast for fear of the serpent, so he asked the serpent to allow him to put a cauldron on her head until Monday. She consented to this, not realising until later that Cuan meant the Monday of Judgement Day. She then spoke a verse saying that if it were not for the cauldron on her head she would devour more than two-thirds of the world. Two men passing by the lake one early spring afternoon mocked the idea of her existence, and she immediately rose up, and the sound of water and ice-breaking could be heard half a mile away.

A variant of this legend says that her back emerges every May Day morning; she cannot put up her head because of the cauldron on it. According to William Gregory Wood-Martin in *Traces of the Elder Faiths of Ireland*, the serpent once devoured both the inhabitants of a nearby fortress and its cattle. In a rare case of cowardice, Cúchulainn, who was close by, said "these be no friends of mine" and jumped over the castle wall in fear.

CATA: PART 1

Cata is the monster that gave the name to Iniscatha, now known as Scattery Island at the mouth of the Shannon river. Cata is first mentioned in the medieval book of Lismore, which tells us that Cata devoured St Senan's smith, named Narach, but that the saint brought him back to life with a miracle. After this St Senan and the beast battled. The Cata advanced, "its eyes flashing flame, with fiery breath, spitting venom and opening its horrible jaws", but Senan made the sign of the cross, and the beast collapsed, making it possible to chain it up and throw it into Doolough, near Mount Callan. There were images of the beast that showed the daemon with a spiked back, scales, fish tail, nose curling up spirally, and clawed forefeet, though these have now been lost.

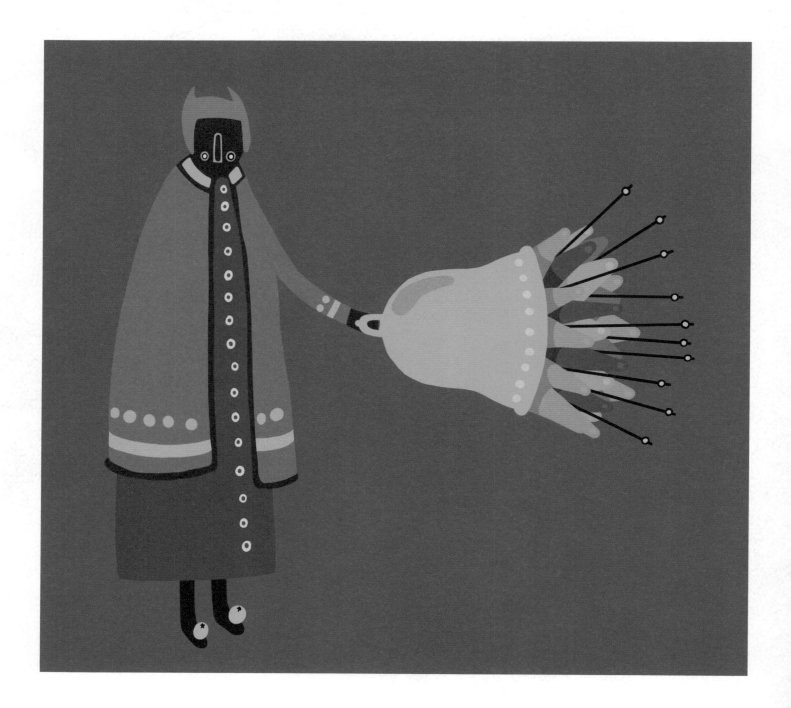

CATA: PART 2

 generation later, St Mac Creiche[1], who is described as a 'dragon queller', and a beast[2] whose name has changed now to Bruckee[3], had their own battle. The beast appeared in Loch Briocsigh[4]. The beast was as tall as a tree and could discharge balls of fire from its mouth. It was on a rampage, attacking and killing people. St Mac Creiche carried a magic bell and shot a ball of fire from it into the beast's mouth, setting it ablaze. He then drove the wounded creature back into the lake, which turned red with the monster's blood. The beast rose again from the lake, which shocked and embarrassed the saint. This time Mac Creiche took off his cloak and threw it over the creature's heads; the cloak grew and grew, like a cloak of melted iron, and this pressed the beast down to the bottom of the lake, where it was not to arise until judgement day. The saint then warned the people that if they did not pay a tribute, they would be cursed with disease pestilence and conflict.

This is the etymology of the place name Poulnabruckee, which was the daemon Bruckee's den near Inchiquin in Co. Clare. There is a 15th century carving in Kilmacreehy of a beast, which could be the Cata/Bruckee.

1. St Mac Creiche is said to be from Liscannor in Co. Clare.
2. The beast's name was formerly Cata.
3. Bruckee can be translated as Broc-Sidhe or 'fairy badger'.
4. The 'fairy badgers' lake', today called Lough Raha.

KERHANAGH/CAORANACH OR 'FIRE SPITTER': PART 1

When St Patrick was driving the peists, daemons and snakes out of Ireland, he first drove them to Ireland's holy mountain of Croagh Patrick. On the northern side of this great seaside rock is a hollow in the mountain called Lugnadaemon, which translates to 'hollow of the demons'. According to legend, this was the last place the daemons retreated before being banished into the sea forever. When St Patrick was herding the daemons towards the sea, one of them, named the Kerhanagh, slipped away and escaped. When St Patrick had finished expelling the creatures on the mountain, he tried to catch the slippery Kerhanagh, but the Kerhanagh stayed ahead of the saint, eventually making his way north toward Sligo.

The daemon spoiled all the wells along the way with his foul fiery breath, until he and St Patrick came to Tullaghan Well in Co. Sligo. At Tullaghan Well, St Patrick was overcome with a great thirst. He prayed for a drink and a fountain sprung up on the side of the little hill. After his thirst was quenched, his strength was renewed and he was able to defeat the daemon, driving her away from Ireland forever.

This well was subsequently held in great veneration to St Patrick, and there is a hollow on the hill where the saint lay concealed until they daemon came into sight.

KERHANAGH/CAORANACH OR 'FIRE SPITTER': PART 2

There is another legend that says that St Patrick failed to kill The Caoranach in Sligo, allowing her to make her way further north, where she is the giant serpent or monster dwelling in the waters of Lough Derg in Co. Donegal. Legend has it that she appears during stormy weather, when she sucks men and cattle into her gaping mouth. Her lair is said to be close to the pilgrimage site of Station Island, and indeed there is a stone there that is said to be part of her skeleton. The name Caoranach could be a derivation of the name Corra, who was an Irish goddess that St Patrick battled with on top of Croagh Patrick.

There is also folklore that suggests that St Patrick fought the creature for two nights and two days while both were submerged in the water.

Another older legend says that when the shinbones of Fionn MacCumhail'sI mother were thrown into Lough Derg, they immediately came alive as The Caoranach, who ate her grandchild Conan, who then fought his way out of her belly. The blood of her dying body turned the lake red, which in turn gave the lake its name Lough Derg.[1]

1. 1. Lough Derg translates as red lake. 'Lake' (Lough) 'Red' (Derg or Dearg).

THE IRISH CYCLOPS

n the legendary Irish story 'The Pursuit of Diarmuid and Grainne', translated by the Ossianic society, there is a legend of a giant cyclops.

In the story, the Tuatha De Danaan wanted to protect a quicken tree, or rowan tree, from the Fenians of Erin.[1] This quicken tree was magical. Any one who ate three berries from it would suffer no disease or sickness, and would feel the exhilaration of wine and the satisfaction of mead, and if they were one hundred years old, anyone who tasted these berries would return again as a thirty-year-old.

The Tuatha sent one of their own, a youth named Searbhan Lochlannach, to guard the tree. He was described as a thick boned, large nosed, crooked tusked, red-eyed, and swarthy bodied giant. He was the child of wicked Cam, son of Naoi.[2] Weapons would not wound him, fire would not burn him, and water would not drown him, so great was his magic. He had but one eye in the middle of his black forehead, and he had a thick collar of iron round his giant body, and he is fated not to die until he is struck with three strokes of the iron club that he carries with him.

Grainne, the heroine of the story, explained to Diarmuid that she would die unless she tasted the magical berries.

Diarmuid had a furious fight, attained the giant's club and delivered three mighty blows, killing the giant. He then presented Grainne with the berries.

1. The Fenians of Erin were a small army associated with the legendary heroic figure Fionn Mac Cumhaill.
2. Cam is a derivation of the name Ham and Naoi is a derivation of the name Noah.

THE SWAN WOMAN

There are many popular stories relating to the swan in Ireland, the most famous of which is 'The Children of Lir'. It was always thought in Ireland that it was unlucky to kill a swan— perhaps this is related to the belief that they held the souls of chaste girls.

It was also thought that a swan could put a person under her spell with the sound of her musical voice.

In P.W. Joyce's *The Wonder of Ireland*, he recounts the folk story of the 10th century poet Erard MacCossi. In the legend, MacCossi[1] saw a flock of swans flying near him on the Boyne river. Erard threw a stone and hit one of the swans on the wing, and it fell to the ground. Erard ran to catch it, but when he reached it he found that it had turned into a woman. He asked how she came to be in the shape of a swan, and she answered him, saying that she was gravely ill and daemons had spirited her away and that it seemed to her companions that she was dead. Both she and the daemons took the shape of swans until the curse was broken by that lucky accident with the poet. Mac Cossi cared for her in his house and after a time returned her to her friends.

There is also a legend involving Oengus.[2] In the legend, Oengus has a dream that lasts over a year. In the dream Princess Caer Ibormeith stood beside his bed, but whenever he reached out to touch her, she disappeared.[3] Caer was enchanted and every alternate year she appeared as either a human or a swan. Oengus searches for her in his dreams and finds her with 149 other girls chained in pairs at 'Loch Bel Dracon'. Oengus is told that if he can identify his Caer in swan form from amongst the 150 swans, he can marry her. Wisely Oengus enchants himself and turns into a swan. In this guise he easily recognises Caer. They fly away together, singing as they go. This sweet singing put all that could hear them to sleep for three days and three nights.

1. The origin of this legend is from the book of Glendalough, which no longer exists, however transcripts from it appear in the 14th century *Book of Balymote*.
2. Oengus is a member of the Tuatha DeDanaan and is the god of love, youth and poetry.
3. Caer Ibormeith was a daughter of Prince Ethal Anbuail of Connaught.

CHROM-DUBH

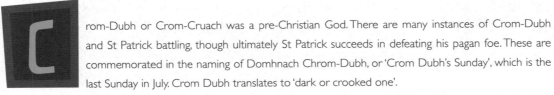

Crom-Dubh or Crom-Cruach was a pre-Christian God. There are many instances of Crom-Dubh and St Patrick battling, though ultimately St Patrick succeeds in defeating his pagan foe. These are commemorated in the naming of Domhnach Chrom-Dubh, or 'Crom Dubh's Sunday', which is the last Sunday in July. Crom Dubh translates to 'dark or crooked one'.

There are many sites around Ireland devoted to Crom Dubh and his battles with St Patrick, and these places often have serpents or daemons associated with them. One, named Mamean, is particularly interesting, and is at a site very close to my own home. In many respects it got me interested in this subject.

Mám-Éan translates as 'pass of the birds', which makes sense as it connects at a height two valleys in Connemara. According to the legend, Crom Dubh is a speckled bull that attacked all who attempted to use the pass. St Patrick fought the bull and drove him into a little lake that to this day is called Loch an Tairbh (the Bull's lake), and has had a red glow on it ever since. This little lake is thought to be bottomless, with an enchanted serpent (oll-Pheist) in it imprisoned by St Patrick.

THE WHITE TROUT OF CONG

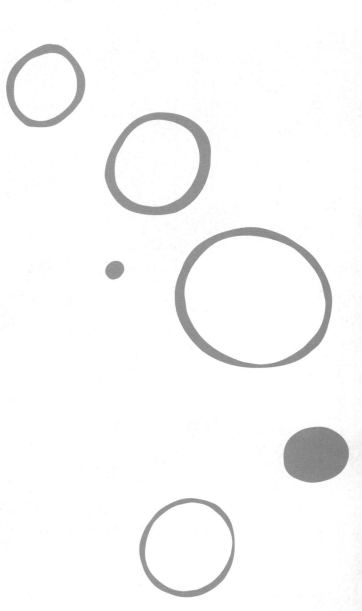

Samuel Lover in his book from the 1830s, *Legends and Stories of Ireland*, recounts a folktale he heard about the white trout of Cong. The story is set in the pigeonhole, which is a natural cave with 61 steps leading down to a subterranean river.

The tale goes that once there was a beautiful girl who was betrothed to a prince, but sadly, before their wedding day the prince was murdered and thrown into the lake. The girl was so distraught at her loss that she hid away. The story goes that the fairies took her away. Over the course of time the white trout was seen in the underground river at the pigeonhole. The white trout lived in the same spot for years and local people knew not to harm it. All was well until some soldiers entered the village, one of whom heard the story of the white trout and was determined to eat it, despite vigorous warnings.

The soldier caught the little white trout and attempted to fry it on a pan, despite its human cries of pain. No matter how long he tried to fry it, it wouldn't cook. Eventually he took his knife to its side. As soon as he put his knife to the fish there was a murderous scream. The trout jumped from the pan into the fire and on the spot where it fell rose up the beautiful girl with blood streaming down her arm. She told the soldier of her murdered fiancée and how she was waiting for him in the stream, and that if she missed him because of the soldier's evil deeds, she would curse him for all time. She then insisted that he return her to the stream so she could resume her vigil. When he saw her in the water he could see the red marks of where he had cut her, which remain on white trout to this day.

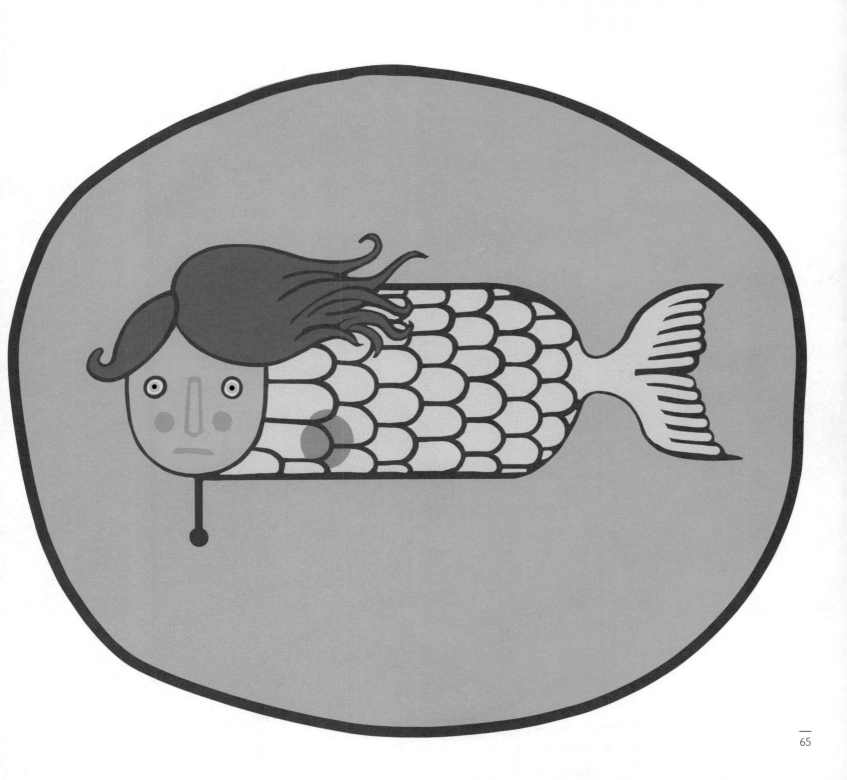

THE LEANHAUN SHEE

The Leanhaun Shee or 'faerie mistress' is the female version of the 'Gancanach'. She seeks out the love of men, and if they refuse her advances she becomes enslaved to them. However, if they consent, they belong to her, and the only escape from such a curse is by finding another man to replace the first. All her lovers waste away, because she is like a parasite feeding on their life-force. Bards in the past were often entranced by the Leanhaun Shee because she also acted as a sort of muse, offering inspiration to her consorts. Ultimately she is like a poisoned chalice; the Irish bards under her spell died young, and after their deaths she would go on to seduce another and another.

KING OF THE CATS

There are many stories connected to the King of the Cats, the most famous of which is of Irusan. Irusan lived in a cave near Clonmacnoise and was as big as an ox. The first mention of Irusan comes from 'Imtheacht na Tromdhaimhe' (The Proceedings of the Great Bardic Institution), which dates back to the 15th century. According to the story, the chief poet of Ireland, Senchan Torpeist, cursed all the mice of Ireland and went on to curse the cats whose job it was to kill the mice. In retribution, Irusan hunted down the poet with the intention of killing him. Irusan caught the poet and held him by the arm. Senchan was afraid for his life and tried to flatter the cat to no avail. Irusan went straight to the forge at Clonmacnoise where St Ciaran happened to be. He was shocked at the poet's plight and killed the cat with a red-hot poker from the fire.

Some say the King of the Cats lives to this day, looking like any other cat. If you wish to verify if a cat has any royal claim, you merely snip a bit of his ear; if he speaks out, declaring who he is, you can be sure you are in the presence of royalty.

A related legend involves Luchtigern, King of the Mice. Luchtigern was the King of the Mice in Kilkenny and was slain by the huge cat monster, Banghaisgidheach, who lived in the Dunmore caves near modern-day Kilkenny city.

The Kilkenny gaelic football team and the hurling team are known as 'The Cats'. This legend comes from a macabre story of cats that got into such frenzied fights that they devoured each other to the point that all that was left were their tails.

THE KING WITH HORSE EARS

 In the crypt of St Patrick's Cathedral in Armagh is a sculpture of a man with the ears of a horse. This is thought to be an adapted version of the tale of King Midas. The Irish version of the story features King Labraidh Loinseach, who was cursed with horse ears. Society at the time wouldn't allow a king with an imperfect body, so in order to protect his secret, he killed his barbers as soon as they cut his hair. When the widowed mother of one of his barbers pleaded with the king to spare her son, he was merciful, on the condition that the barber would never reveal the king's secret. Over time, this became such a hardship for the boy that it made him ill. In order to relieve himself of this burden, he confessed his secret to a willow tree, and he was cured. In time this tree was cut and its timber was used to make a magic harp. When this magical harp was played in the king's court, it sang out and revealed the king's secret horse ears.

MECHI

Mechi is the son of the Morrigan. We can find the mythology of Mechi in the Dindshenchas, which is a 12th century manuscript.

Mechi was born with three hearts, and living in each heart was a snake. There was a prophesy that unless Mechi was killed, the snakes would 'have grown in his belly until they would not have left an animal alive in Ireland'. MacCecht,[1] who was known as 'the slayer of a hundred', killed Mechi and afterward removed the hearts and burned them on MagLuathat, which translates to 'the plain of ashes'. MacCecht then cast the ashes into the Barrow River, which boiled until the ashes dissolved.

1. MacCecht shared the kingship of Ireland with his brothers. They rotated their kingship between them a year at a time, covering around thirty years.

GANCANACH

ancanach, from the Irish gean canach, meaning 'love talker' is a male fairy in Irish mythology that is known for seducing women.

The Gancanach was a solitary faerie like the Leprechaun. He was devoted to idleness and always appeared with a little clay pipe called a duidin. He was often spotted in lonesome places and had a particular affection for shepherdesses and milkmaids. If someone fell for him, he would ultimately abandon them and they would pine for death! It was said that anyone who lost their fortune from devotion to a woman was said to have met a Gancanach. It is interesting to note that the poet W. .B. Yeats used the Gancanach as a *nom de plume* in his book *John Sherman and the Dhoya*.

GLAS GOIBHNEANN

G las Goibhneann translates as the Grey Cow of Goibhneann. The grey cow of Goibhneann was a magical or fairy cow guarded by the craftsman Goibhneann, who kept the halter to which she unfailingly returned every night. There are many stories in Irish folklore relating to this bountiful animal. She was so strong she could walk through three of Ireland's provinces in one day, and her milk was so plentiful that she could feed hundreds of people with it.

One story about this amazing cow was that at one milking, she could fill any vessel, no matter how large. Two women wagered on whether a vessel could be found to outsize her capacity, and when a sieve was produced, the ever-flowing cow's milk caused seven streams to overflow. Also it was said "the hoofs of this cow were reversed", and the backward tracks always fooled the potential cattle-thieves in pursuit.

In the Burren, in Co. Clare, there is supposedly a swallow hole named Poll Leamhnachta, which translates to 'hole of sweet milk'. It is here that, even with the grey cow's endless supply of milk, she could not fill the hole, and disappeared in the attempt.

DULLAHAN OR DULACHAN

T he Dullahan are headless phantoms that are widespread around Ireland, though variants of them can be found around Europe and as far away as the Americas. Sometime they are women but more often they are men. Sometimes the Dullahan is referred to as 'Gan Ceann', without a head.

The Dullahan are seen with headless horses and coiste-bodhar, or the coach-a-bower, which is an immense black funeral coach mounted with a coffin.[1] These phantoms can carry their own heads in their arms. If you hear the sound of a coach, be sure not to open the door because if you open it, the Dullahan will throw a basin of blood in your face. His eyes are dark and always darting around. If the Dullahan sees you looking at him, he will whip your eyes out.

There are numerous stories of the Dullahan in Ireland and some that connect the death coach to fairies.

People used to be taken by the fairies long ago, and it seems they lived out their ordinary span of life among the fairies. When they died and they had to be buried, people said that this death coach was the hearse that was used for them by the fairy people.

There is also a link between the Dullahan and gold. In Co. Roscommon there was a tradition that if you carried a piece of gold it would frighten the Dullahan away. In Connemara, a folklorist reinforced this idea when he recorded that somebody having dropped their gold headed pin scared the Dullahan away.

1. Coiste-bodhar translates to 'road coach'.

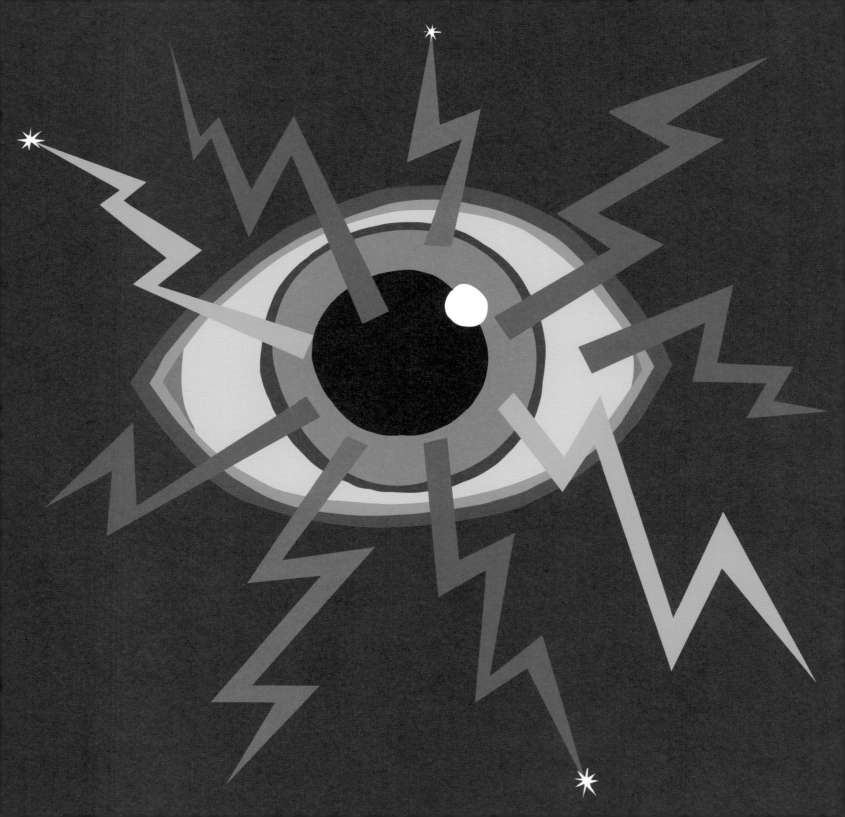

BALOR OF THE EVIL EYE: THE IRISH CYCLOPS

Balor was the King of the Fomorians,[1] and came from a great castle on Tory Island in Donegal. He was a giant with a basilisk[2] eye that he only opened when in battle. This eye could kill with a single glance and took four men to open it. Balor received his poisonous eye as a child, when he spied on his father's druids making potions of death; some of the fumes from the concoction went into his eye, creating the magic. On the same day, one of the druids gave a prophesy that Balor would be killed by his own grandson. Balor went to some lengths to prevent the prophesy of his death from coming true. He locked his daughter Eithne in a tower, but despite this, ultimately it was himself who caused Eithne to meet the man that would father his grandson.

Balor coveted the faerie cow 'Glas Ghoibheann', of whom we have an entry in this book, and stole her while he was in disguise. Cian, who was a member of the Tuatha De Danaan, was guarding the cow and when he went to retrieve it, he met Eithne, and from their union Eithne bore a son, Lugh.[3]

Lugh became the King of the Tuatha de Danaan and lead them in the second battle of Moyturra against the Formorian army led by Balor. Lugh killed Balor by piercing his evil eye with a spear that was crafted by Goibnu, the owner of the faerie cow. A legend from Sligo mentions that Lough na Suil, which means, 'lake of the eye', was created when Balor fell face down after being killed by Lugh; his evil eye burned a crater in the earth which filled with water, and so the lake was created.

1. The Fomorians were evil giants that came from the sea.
2. The word basilisk refers to legendary creatures that could use their eyes to kill people with just a glance.
3. Tuatha DeDanaan, are the people or tribe of the goddess Danaan. They are a supernatural race in Irish mythology.

LI BAN MERMAID

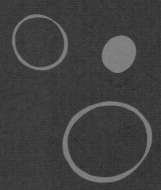

The first mention of Li Ban comes from the Annals of the Four Masters.[1] In the Annals it is written that a mermaid was found ashore in Scotland. She was 195 feet in length, her hair was eighteen feet long, her fingers were seven feet as was her nose and she was as white as a swan. In this extract she gets her nickname Muirgheilt or 'sea lunatic'.

The more popular legend is that she was the human daughter of the King of Tara.[2] She was baptised in the 6th century by St Comgall, who was the bishop of Bangor in Co. Down. According to the legend, she lived near what is now Lough Neagh in Northern Ireland. She was swept away when someone failed to cover a sacred well.[3] The well overflowed, killing all her family and destroying their kingdom. Only Li ban survived with her dog as she was caught in an underwater bubble, where they dwelled for two years. From there she saw the swimming salmon and prayed to become one. Her prayers were answered and she gained the body of a salmon while retaining her human head. Her little dog became an otter. She was free to wander the seas, while retaining her home in Lough Neagh.

After 300 years she was 'saved' after being baptised so she could ascend into heaven. Li Ban came to be known as the mermaid of Lough Neagh. She is also venerated as St Muirgen, 'sea born'.

1. *The Annals of the Four Masters* is a compilation of earlier books, although they contain some original work. They were written in the north west of Ireland in the 1630s. The annals are written in Irish. Several manuscript copies are held at Trinity College Dublin, the Royal Irish Academy, University College Dublin and the National Library of Ireland.

2. Tara is a hill in Co. Meath. Tara was the ancient seat of power, and the King of Tara was considered to be of ultimate authority in Ireland.

3. Lough Neagh (old Irish: Loch nEchach) is named after Li Ban's father, Eochaid Mac Mairidh.

LUTUR

The story of Lutur is a curious one. It comes from poem 8 in the 12th century book *Dindshenchas*.

This myth features Lutur and Gablach. Lutur is described as being higher than any oak tree and that he comes from the western side of Spain. He came to Ireland to woo Gablach, who is described as being fifty cubits tall and half of that in breadth. Gablach welcomed her suitor and they had a feast that is described as having a hundred of 'every beast' and a hundred measures of every grain on earth. The following morning they were awoken by Fuither[1] and his army, who had also come to woo Gablach. Fuither shouted "Come out of your own accord, or else by force!"

Lutur came out fighting. He had a large stake of timber with which he attacked, crushing their heads and leaving pools of 'blood and brains'. When Lutur and his fourteen heads and Fuither grew tired, Gablach attacked and killed Fuither and his army, not one of whom escaped with their life. From this story came the name Dun Gabail, which translates to the 'Fort of Gabail', on the River Liffey.

1.   Fuither came from the islands of the Red Sea.

PUCA POOKA

The Pooka is a well-known spirit in the Irish tradition that could change shape. The Pooka could be a goat, horse, donkey, eagle or even a black dog. The Pooka rarely takes human form, but when it does it can retain some animal features such as the ears of a donkey or the tail of a horse. This spirit is considered mostly malevolent. He loves to take innocent mortals for dangerous rides through the countryside on his back, only to shake them off the following morning. The Pooka particularly likes to prank drunkards, for as W. B. Yeats put it, "A drunkards sleeps in his kingdom". There is a legend that Brian Boru[1] was the only man to ever successfully ride a pooka, and this he did with the aid of a magic bridle.

The 1st of November is sacred to the pooka, and people will always be safe from them on that day. In the countryside, children are told not to eat any blackberries that were overripe as this was a sign that the pooka had spat on them. College students in Ireland that wear predominantly black are often referred to as pookies in reference to the black pooka.

---

1. Brian Boru was born in Co. Clare in 941 AD. He was the last High King of Ireland (i.e. the last king to rule the whole Island of Ireland).

THE BANSHEE: PART 1

The literal translation of Banshee from the Irish is 'woman fairy'. She is the fairy death messenger, or the spirit of death. This creature is most closely associated with old Irish families whose surnames began with a Mac or an O', and if they heard her cry it was thought death was sure to follow, for it is said that the cry of the Banshee was a harbinger of death in the family.

There are many accounts of the Banshee in folklore, but the most prevalent seems to be an association with keening. Keening was an Irish funeral tradition where woman would congregate and cry in grief at a funeral, a service they were often paid for. Like Irish mermaids, the Banshee is often associated with a comb of silver or gold, though there is a story from Co. Laois that says the comb is actually made from bone.

One story from Lady Wilde's book recounts the story of a noble Irish lady in her death bed. The gravely ill woman opens her eyes and points to the window. All in attendance look to the window but nothing was there. They then heard the sweetest music coming from the window and echoing all around the house. Many who were there thought it was a trick and searched the grounds, but nothing human was seen. All the while the plaintive music was being sung and did not cease for the entire night. The next morning the noblewoman lay dead and the music had ceased.

How the Banshee looks is open to interpretation, as there are many differing reports. More often than not her eyes are red from crying and her mouth open in a wail. She wears grey at night and she has been described as a beautiful maiden weeping at an impending death, or a gruesome hag foretelling it.

THE BANSHEE: PART 2

s was written in the first part of the Banshee, the name translates as woman fairy. There are some names very closely associated with the Banshee. Aoibheall is a fairy queen from Co. Clare and is the Banshee associated with the O'Brien family. The name Aoibheall means 'beautiful'. The most renowned Banshee is probably Cliodhna, who had a palace in Carrigcleena close to Mallow in Co. Cork. Her tale is a sad one. It was said that she had left her faery land to visit her mortal lover Ciabhan. Manannan Mac Lir, the god of the sea, played her music to send her to sleep on her travels. As she fell asleep on the strand[1] a wave took her. Sometimes among the caves and cliffs there is a very unusual sound, a deep, hollow and melancholy roar, the sound was thought to foretell the death of a king from the south of Ireland. This unusual sound has been called 'Tonn-Cleena', 'Cleena's wave.'

1. Glandore Harbour, Co. Cork.

GLARCUS THE GIANT

G alrcus was a giant of enormous size. In an extract from the book, *The Life of St Patrick*, the writer Colgan describes a meeting between St Patrick and this giant.

St Patrick was travelling around Connaught with his companions when they came across a tomb of astonishing size (30 feet long). St Patrick's followers believed that no man could ever have needed a grave so big. The Saint replied that God, by the resurrection of the giant, could persuade them that such a creature could exist. St Patrick prayed fervently and then, suddenly, up rose the giant from the grave. The giant thanked St Patrick for saving him from the gates of hell, where he had been suffering unspeakable torments. His name was Glarcus, son of Chais, and he was killed one hundred years previously by Fionn MacCumhaill, during the reign of King Cairbre. He requested to follow St Patrick, but he was refused because Patrick's disciples could not bear to look at him without being terrified. St Patrick then baptised him, allowing him to avoid the gates of hell.

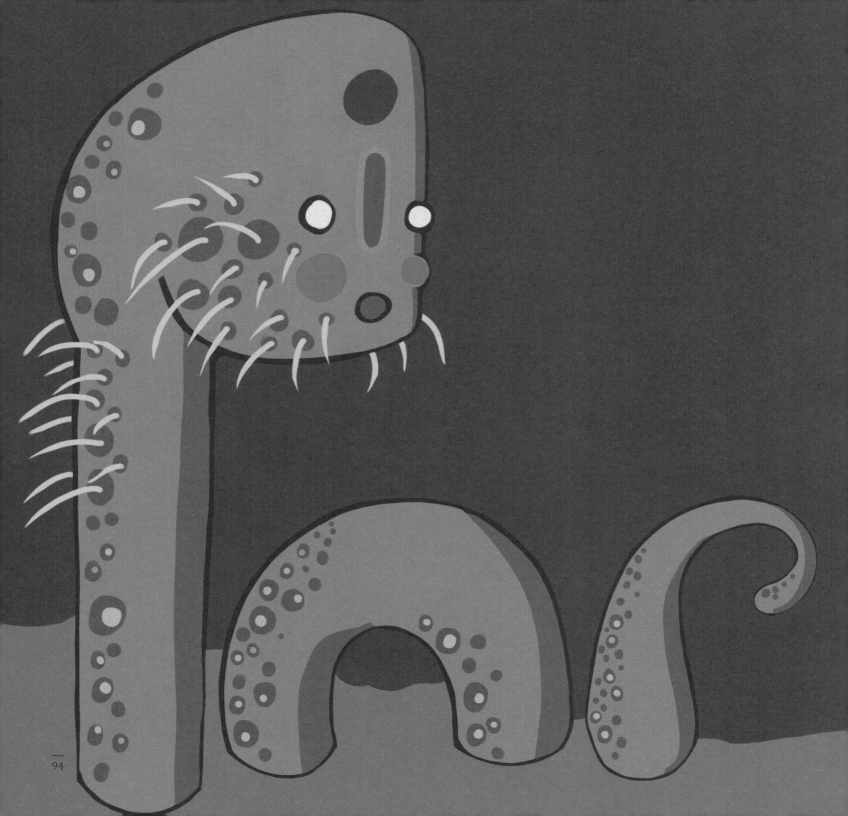

MONSTER FROM THE RIVER NESS

he first ever mention of 'The Loch Ness Monster' comes from the 'Vita Columba' or 'Life of Columba', which was written by the Adomnán, who served as the ninth Abbot of Iona until his death in 704 A.D. I am including it in this book because St Columba is Irish. According to Adomnán, Columba came across a group of Scottish men burying a man beside the river Ness. He had been killed by a monster. Columba then sent one of his followers across the river, but the monster began to approach this man. Columba made the sign of the cross and cried out, "Thou shalt go no further, nor touch the man; go back with all speed." The beast was shocked and retreated, terrified, to the lake. The Scottish men gathered around and were amazed and hence glorified Columba's God. Whether or not this incident is true, Adomnan's text specifically states that the monster was swimming in the River Ness – the river flowing from the loch – rather than in Loch Ness itself.

FOMORIAN GIANT: 'FOVOR-OF-THE-BLOWS'

he Fomorians[1] were generally considered a malevolent and supernatural race of Gods. It is also thought that they were an early race of sea raiders or pirates.

In one Irish myth story[2] it is written that the Princess Niamh of Tir na Nog was held captive by the Fomorian Giant Fovor.[3] The hero of the story is Oisin,[4] and when he met Niamh he swore to free her from the evil giant.

Niamh is described as golden haired with clear blue eyes and lips the colour of berries.

Not long after Oisin met Niamh, the giant approached and declared battle of a mighty single fight. Oisin met Fovor head on and over the course of three days and three nights they fought. The battle was tough and the giant a worthy adversary, but at last Oisin cut the giant's head off with his sword 'Ceard nan Gallen'.[5]

1. For more information on The Fomorians, see page 111.
2. *The Lay of Oisin in the Land of Youth* by Micheal Coimin, 1750.
3. Tir na Nog is a mythical island which translates as 'the land of youth' and its inhabitants do not age.
4. Oisin is the son of Sadhbh (see page 100) and Fionn MacCumhaill and his name means 'young deer'.
5. Oisin's sword is named 'Ceard nan Gallan' which translates to 'the smith of the branches'.

BAN NAEMHA, WHO COULD TELL THE FUTURE

There is a well in Co. Cork called Tober Kil-na-Greina, which translates to 'the well of the church of the sun'.

According to legend, a woman called Ban-na-Naomha lived by a magic stone and well, and she had the gift of telling the future. St Patrick cursed this pagan site and turned the land around it into a marsh. For hundreds of years the well and marsh lay dormant until an enterprising farmer removed the stone, which could hold water, and used it as a drinking trough for his cattle. In time his cattle got sick, and then his children. The farmer returned the stone and drained the land, after which a spring of fresh water that had lain hidden for a thousand years sprang up (and all his household were cured).

According to Lady Wilde who wrote of the site in 1887:

"The ritual observed was very strict at the beginning, three draughts of water were taken by the pilgrims, the number of drinks three, the number of rounds on their knees were three, thus making the circuit of the well nine times. After each round the pilgrim laid a stone on the ancient altar in the Druid circle, called 'the well of time sun', and these stones, named in Irish 'the stones of the sun', are generally pure white, and about the size of a pigeon's egg. They have a beautiful appearance after rain when the sun shines on them, and were doubtless held sacred to the sun in pagan times. The angels will reckon these stones at the last day, but each particular saint will take charge of his own votaries and see that the stones are properly counted, for each man will receive forgiveness according to their number."

People continued to observe the tradition until a man was killed and the curative properties were lost. The woman, Ban-Naomha, or the nymph of the fountain, who used to appear occasionally in the form of a trout, disappeared at this time, though she may be at other sacred wells. The trout is a common reference. Many holy wells are said to contain blessed fish, examples can be seen in the story of Li-ban or the white trout of Cong. Other times they may be eels or salmon. Seeing one was considered extremely lucky and a good omen that your prayers would be heard.

SADHBH

he mythical hero Fionn, leader of the Fianna, was out hunting with his dogs Bran and Sceolaing when they came across a young fawn. To Fionn's surprise, the dogs went up to it and gently began to lick it. The fawn followed them home to Eamain Macha and Sadhbh returned to her human form. The fawn, now in human form, explained to Fionn that she was enchanted by the Fear Doirche, or 'dark man', because she refused his advances. Fionn and Sadhbh were soon married. Some time after, while Fionn was away hunting, Sadhbh was kidnapped by the Fear Doirche.

Unbeknownst to Fionn, she was pregnant. Fionn spent the next seven years searching for her without success. Sadly, no legend records what happened to Sadhbh. However, once, while searching, his dogs found a wild young boy who Fionn recognised as his own son, whom he called Oisin, which translates to young deer. As Oisin grew he came to be known as the greatest poet of Ireland and had many great adventures.

RUCHT AND FRIUCH: AN EPIC BATTLE BETWEEN TWO SHAPE SHIFTERS

R ucht and Friuch must be two of the most prodigious shapeshifters in Ireland. This tale is taken from the epic Irish story 'The Cattle Raid of Cooley' and has its origin in the 12th century *Book of the Dun Cow* .

The story goes that there were two pig keepers named Rucht, 'boar's grunt', and Friuch, 'boar's whiskers'. Rucht was from Connaught and Friuch was from Munster. They could both perform the pagan arts and enchant themselves into any animal. They were friends, and as such if there was extra food in the south, Rucht would travel down without hindrance from his friend to share in the bounty.

However, things weren't to remain cordial. The next time Rucht went south, he and Friuch argued about who was the most powerful. Friuch said, "I'll cast a spell over your pigs. Even though they eat as much as mine they won't grow fat, while mine will." This spell came true and when Friuch went north, Rucht cast the same spell on his own pigs, which also came to pass. As a result, the men's respective kings dismissed them. After the two pig keepers were dismissed they spent the next two years shapeshifting, first fighting as birds, named Talon and Wing, and two years under the sea fighting as sea creatures, named Whale and Seabeast; one in the Shannon and the other in the Suir. Then they became two stags, then two warriors, Point and Edge, then two phantoms, Shadow and Shield, then two dragons, pouring snow on each other's land, then two worms and finally two bulls, Donn Cuailnge and Finnbhennach.[1]

1. Friuch in the guise of the bull Donn Cuailnge is the central part of the Irish legend 'The Cattle Raid of Cooley'.

ELLEN TRECHEND

ath Croaghan is a very important site in Irish mythology that is sometimes referred to as Oweynagat or 'cave of the cats'. It is thought that the 'King of the Cats' lives here. It is also considered to be the gate to the underworld of Ireland. Ellen Trechend is mentioned as a mythical three-headed monster that emerged from this cave and lay waste to all the land, withering all the crops of Ulster. It continued its rampage until it was killed by Amergin, the poet who fostered Cúchulainn. Ellen Trechend is a difficult name to translate, and different translators have different interpretations. It could be described as a swarm of three headed creatures, a monstrous three-headed bird or even a fire-breathing monster.

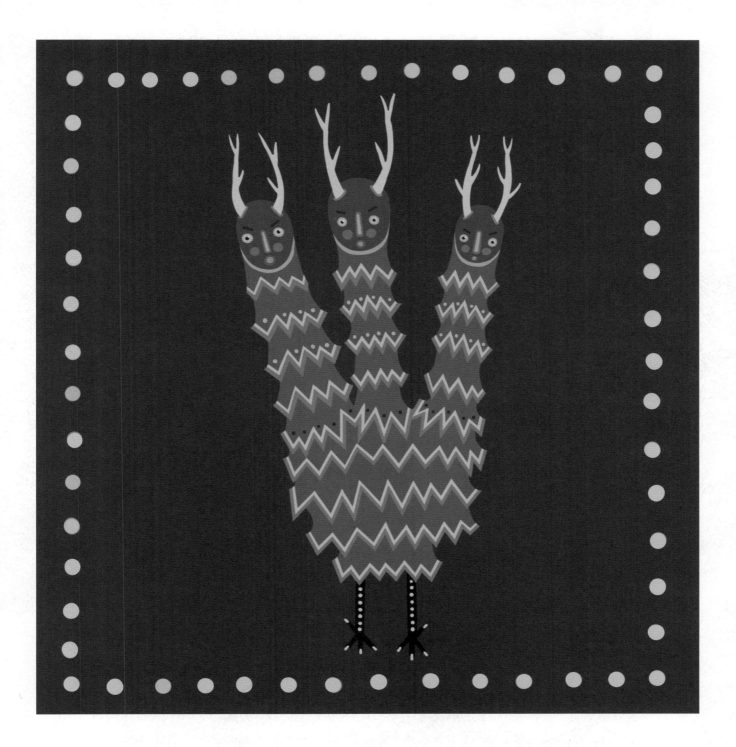

AILLEN MACMIDGNA

Aillen lived in Magh Meall, which is a kind of magical realm that was thought to be an island to the west of Ireland. On this island, death did not exist and in many respects it was similar to Tír na nÓg. Aillen was known as 'The Burner' and could spit huge flames of fire. He was also the fairy musician of the Tuatha DeDanaan[1] and every Samain (Halloween) he would visit the hill of Tara playing his music on the 'tiompan',[2] which would magically send its inhabitants to sleep. Aillen would then use the power of his fire breath to burn Tara to the ground, which he did for twenty-three years, and every year they would rebuild. Finally, the hero Fionn MacCumhaill arrived. He made himself immune to the power of the sleeping music by ingesting a poison that would inhibit sleep. Fionn then proceeded to kill Aillen with his magic spear.

1. Tuatha DeDanaan, People or tribe of the goddess Danaan. They are a supernatural race in Irish mythology
2. The Tiompan was a very ancient Irish musical instrument, which is described in the introduction of the *Transactions of the Ossianic Society, vol. 2,* 1854.

LOCH BEL DRACON

rom the Dindshenchas we get an understanding of the place name of Crotta Cliach. Sliabh Crotta Cliach translates to 'mountains of the harps of Cliach'. Cliach Crotta Cliach is the ancient name for the Galtee Mountains in Co. Tipperary. Cliach was a harper and was sent on behalf of the King of the Three Rosses in Connaught to invite Bodb's daughter Baine to his kingdom.[1] Cliach played music near her fairy hill, however Bodb's magic prevented his music from wooing her. Cliach continued to play his harp for a year, until beneath him the earth cracked open and a dragon burst out. Cliach died of terror, and the lake there is now called Loch Bel Dracon ('the lake of the dragons mouth', now known as Lake Muskry in Co. Tipperary). St Fursey subsequently drove the dragon back into the lake, and there is a prophesy that the dragon will arise again on St John's day at the end of the world and afflict Ireland in vengeance for the death of John the Baptist.

1.   Bodb Dearg translates to Red Bodb. He was King of the Tuatha De Danaan.

THE FOMORIANS

We have already explained legends pertaining to some individual Fomorians like Balor of the evil eye and the giant Searbhan. It should be noted that the Fomorians in general were a malevolent and supernatural race of gods. It is also thought that they were an early race of sea raiders or pirates. The first mention of the Fomorians is from the Lebor Gabála[1] and their fierce chieftain Cichol. They are described as being a race of giants, often with goat or horse-like heads and sometimes with just one eye, one arm and one leg. Early invaders of Ireland were the goat-headed Gaborchend tribe. They may have their origins with the Fomorians.

The name Fomorian could mean something like 'the undersea ones'. One of the great leaders of the Fomorians was Tethra, and he died in the second battle of Moytura.[2]

After Tethra died he became king of the mythical island of Mag Mell. Mag Mell means 'the plain of joy' and only a select few were allowed entry, through death and glory. Mag Mell was a paradise and was inhabited by Irish heroes. Only a few living adventurers visited this paradise, one of which is the Kerry-born St Brendan.

The Fomorians are the enemy of the Ireland's first settlers, the Tuatha De Danaan.[3]

1. Lebor Gabála is a medieval Irish text that translates as 'The Book of the Taking of Ireland'. It is held in Trinity College Dublin.
2. Moytura translates to 'plain of towers'. There were two great battles of Moyturra. The second battle was between the Fomorians and the Tuatha De Danaan.
3. Tuatha De Danaan can be translated as 'The Tribe of the Goddess Dana'.

ÉIS ÉNCHENN

É is Énchenn is a bird-headed woman who commands a troop of similar monstrous bird-headed creatures. We encounter Éis Énchenn when Cúchulainn is attempting to leave his teacher of battle arts, Scáthac. When Cúchulainn meets a one-eyed hag on a narrow walkway, she instructs him to move out of her way; when he complies, she attempts to push him down the cliff, but Cúchulainn succeeds by leaping back onto the walkway and chopping off the hag's head. It is only at this point that she is revealed as Éis Énchenn, the bird-headed mother of three warriors, Ciri, Bir and Blicne, who were to die at the hands of Cúchulainn.

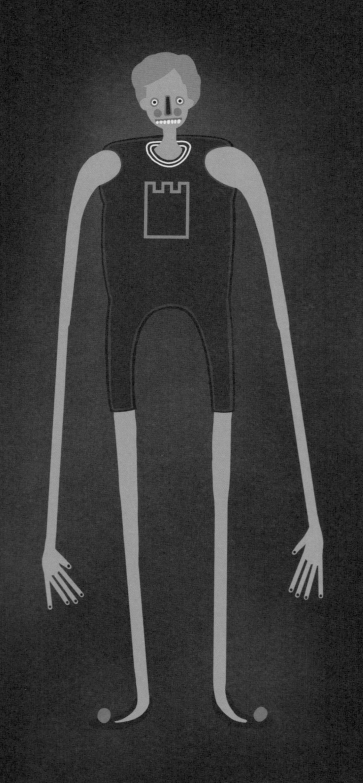

FEAR LIATH

Irish folklore shares many traditions with Scotland, and the Fear Liath or 'grey man' is a good example. The Fear Liath is a malignant creature. His physical manifestation is that of mist or fog, and he can cover the land or sea with his foggy cloak. He does this so that unsuspecting journeymen will tumble to their deaths or ships will run ashore or smash into rocks. He is an ominous presence in Scotland and is said to haunt the summit of Ben Macdhui. When not in the guise of mist he has been described as over ten feet tall, having sallow skin, with broad shoulders and long arms.

There is reference to the Fear Liath on the Sliabh Mish Mountains in Co. Kerry. A man is often seen in the distance with a black dog, but as the climber comes nearer the two creatures disappear, only to be spotted higher up. Many have seen them, but no one has ever been able to meet them. Lady Francesca Wilde recounts in her book[1] the story of a man climbing alone on the mountains.[2] He stopped awhile to take some snuff when he heard a voice call "Not yet! Not yet! I am near you, wait!" He looked about but no one was there. He thought the creature was benign so he took some snuff[3] from the box into his hand. He was shocked when he felt the invisible fingers of the Fear Liath picking at the snuff in his hand. And when he looked down, the snuff had disappeared.

"God and the saints between us and harm!" said the man. Amen said the invisible speaker. The man quickly headed home unharmed.

1. *Ancient Legends, Mystic Charms and Superstition of Ireland,* 1887.
2. Lady Francesca Wilde is the mother of the famous Irish writer and wit Oscar Wilde.
3. Snuff is a powder form of tobacco.

ST FURSEY

St Fursey is a 7th century saint that has a much greater devotion on the continent than in his own native Ireland. He founded a monastery on the small island of Inchagoill on Lough Corrib in Co.. Galway. There is a legend that by the power of prayer he raised two children from the dead. I have decided to include him because he became well known for his visions of monsters and demons, and indeed one demon was thrown at him during his trance and burned him. This story was recorded by the Venerable Bede and is thought to have influenced the *Divinia Commedia* by Dante. St Fursey is also mentioned in relation to the Loch Bel Dracon, mentioned earlier.

THE HAWK OF ACHILL

In this book we have already met the immortal crane that resided on an island off the coast of Co. Mayo. The hawk of Achill is also long lived. We meet him in a dialogue with Fintan. MacBóchra This dialogue was written in Old Irish by an unknown cleric around the 8th or 9th century. In English it is known as 'The Colloquy Between Fintan and the Hawk of Achill'.

The hawk's name was Seabhag, which is Irish for 'hawk'. Fintan, who could speak the language of the bird, explained that he has lived for over 5,500 years since the biblical flood. Fintan explained that he had once lived as a one-eyed salmon, because a hawk took his other eye. Seabhag admitted it was him who stole the eye, and that he was the same age as Fintan. Fintan then recounted that he was blind for 500 years, that he was turned into an eagle for 50 years and then 100 years as a blue-eyed falcon. Finally, the 'King of the Sun' returned him to the shape of a man.

The hawk explained that he was king of the birds and witnessed many of the same events as Fintan. He also said that it was he who killed the solitary cranes of Magh Leana[1] and Inis Geidh.[2] Finally, the hawk told Fintan that he would die the next day. Fintan responded that he should not be concerned as his soul will go to heaven and that he also is destined to die the next day.

1. Magh Leana is the site of a great battle in Co. Offaly
2. Inis Geidh translates as the 'Iniskeas' off the coast of Mayo. According to legend, this is the final resting place of the 'Children of Lir'.

GENITI-GLINNI

The Geniti-glinni were sprite of the valley who kept company with the Deamhan Aeir[1] and were known to inhabit lonely glens and valleys. There is a story connected to them involving Cuchulainn. The story goes that the old chieftain Samera sent three of his warriors to battle the Geniti-glinni that were living in a nearby valley to find the hero he needed. Laegaire was the first to attack, but the sprites retaliated with such a barrage that he was lucky to escape with his life. Conall Cernach was the second to attack these ferocious creatures but he didn't fare much better. Finally Cuchulainn went to battle the creatures, but their shrieks and cries almost deafened him and they tore his clothes and attacked him without restraint. Cuchulainn was about to yield when his faithful charioteer Loeg started to reproach him for cowardice, since one of Loeg's duties was to admonish his master when he saw signs of capitulation. Loeg's admonishments angered Cuchulainn so much that he turned on the evil sprites once more and proceeded to "crush and hack them to pieces, so that the valley ran red with their blood".

1.   Deamhan Aeir or demon of the air taunts the children of Lir. According to P.W. Joyce the Bocanachs (male goblins) and Bananachs (females) were often in the company of the 'Deamhan Aeir'.

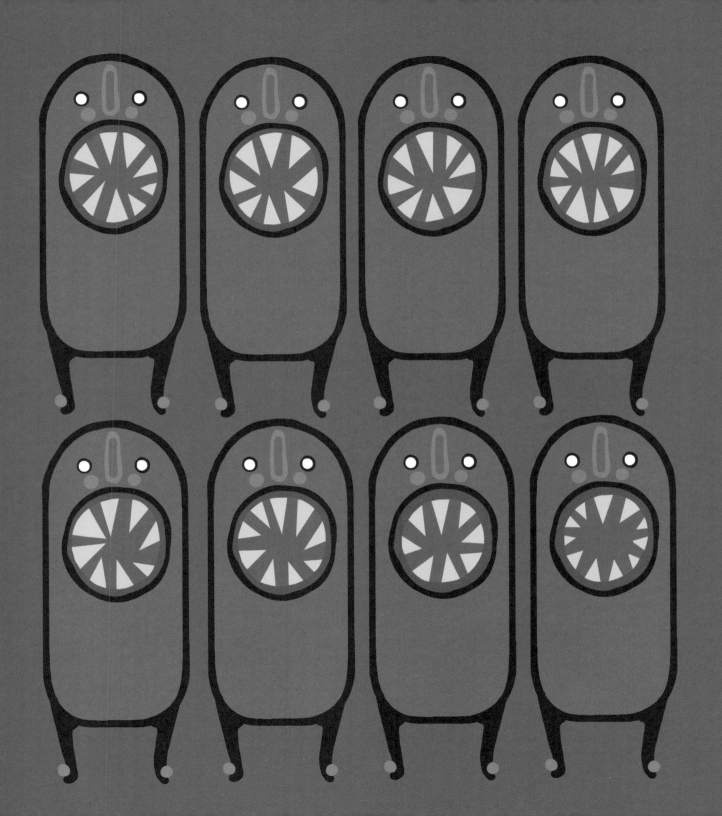

CONCLUSION

The sources for this book are plenty. *The Dindshencas* is a 12th century book giving us the origin of many ancient place names in Ireland, as well as giving us mythical creatures like Iutur or Mechi. We are also lucky to have the translations of medieval books courtesy of The Ossianic Society, who focused on translations from the Fenian period of Irish history. It is from this that we get the translation of 'Ard-na-g-Cath' by Mr John O'Daly.

W. B. Yeats, one of Irelands leading 20th century poets, was enthralled with the legends and folklore of Ireland. Once, while collecting folklore, he famously asked an old man in Co. Sligo "Have you ever seen a fairy or such like?" "Amn't I annoyed with them" was the answer. Yeats wrote many wonderful works based on Irish myth and legend. The Song of Wandering Aengus features an enchanted fish much like 'Li Ban' or 'The White trout of Cong'. In his 1891 book *John Sherman and the Dhoya* Yeats creates his own contemporary mythological giant. The Connemara Giant is another contemporary myth, this time created on a whim by the author. The Connemara Giant is a monumental statue situated in the village of Recess. The legend associated with it claims that if you touch his hand you will be imbued with the knowledge of his ancient tribe.

My hope is that this little book will be like touching the giant's hand and that this will become an introduction to the wealth of myth and legend Ireland has to offer.

I have decided to include an excerpt of 'The Finnian Hunt of Sliabh Truim', for the reason that this portion of the poem is indicative of the genesis of many of the beasts that inhabit the mountain valleys, lakes and rivers of Ireland.

ARD-NA-G-CATH

LAY OF THE CHASE OF SLIABH TRUIM

Edited by Nichlas O'Kearney, Esq. for Transactions of the Ossianic
Society, Vol 2, 1854

When we had disposed of the produce of the chace,
We, the battalions of the ruddy countenances.
The Fenians of Fionn, marched onward
From Sliabh Truim to Loch Cuan.'

We found a piast in the lake ;
Little we profited by being there ;
We cast a glance as we approached,
And saw its head was larger than a hill

It resembled a great mound.
Its jaws were yawning wide;
There might lie concealed, though great its fury,
A hundred champions in its eye-pits.

Longer than any tree in the forest
Were its most formidable tusks ;
Wider than the gates of a city,
Were the ears of the serpent that approached us,

Taller in height than eight men,
Was its tail which was erect above its back;
Thicker was the most slender part of its tail.
Than the forest oak which was sunk by the flood

When it saw before it the hosts.
It prepared itself—and great was its fury;
The lot fell upon Mac Moirne, without mistake,
To engage in the combat with his heroes and hounds.

FIONN. Thou art not one of the Piasts of Eire,
Thou despicable thing without shape or form
Whence hast thou come to the glen?
Asked Fionn the liberal and brave.

PIAST. I have just come hither from Greece
In my course, till I reached Loch Cuan,
To demand battle from the Fenians,
And to annihilate their hosts.

I have subdued every land.
Hosts have fallen by my prowess
Unless from you I do obtain my wish (in conflict),
I will not leave a remnant of you alive.

Give me battle speedily.
You great hosts who are with Fionn
Till I try upon you now
My strength after crossing the wave.

FIONN. By thy love for hospitality relate to us.
Though great thy feats and thy hideousness
The history of thy father and mother.
Before we cast our weapons against thee.

PIAST. An everliving monster that is in Greece,
I shall tell you without deceit his usual name
Crom of the Rook, of great fame.
Who dwells at a rock on the eastern sea.

A piast of great valour but of hideous aspect.
Is his wife without fault
Few are the cities in the east she did not break
And I was born to him as son.

I entailed woe upon every country,
Ard-na-g-Cath is truly my name ;
O Fionn, whose repute and prowess is great,
I care not for thy hosts or their arms.

There is the story thou didst demand from me,
O Fionn, renowned for sword and arms
Come, answer me in conflict speedily.
Though numerous thy hosts and thy strength.

Fionn commanded, though hard the emergency.
The Fenians to meet him in conflict
To repulse him the hosts advanced.
And they met from him a great captivity.

The piast attacked our battalions.
And many of our chieftains by it fell
Great was our- loss in the conflict.
We could not with it contend.

Let the memory of the chace remain on record.
Said the piast vigorous and stout
We cast upon it great showers
Of fire, of darts, and of spears.

By it we were left weak and sick,
We gained no eclat in the contention
It swallowed (though the exertion was great)
Heroes in mail and arms

It swallowed Fionn into its bowels.
The Fenians of Eire raised a shout
We were for a while without help.
And the piast making havoc among us.

An opening on each side of its body
Was made by Fionn, whose mind was not ill
By which he let out without delay
Every one of the Fenians it had swallowed.

Fionn the liberal, from the fight he made,
Saved the hosts at that time;
He liberated us by the might of his hand,
(And) by the powers of his victorious dart.

The Fenians all engaged in the fight.
It required great bravery to conquer it;
They fought, though hard the contest.
Until the vital spark its body left.
Of all the piasts that fell by Fionn,

The number never can be told;
The exploits and achievements he performed.
There is no person who can recount.

He killed the piast of Loch Cuillinn,
It fell by Mac Cumhaill with success;
And the great piast of Binn-eadair,
That was never overcome in battle.

The other piast of Loch Cuillinn,
Fell by Mac Cumhaill of the gold
He slew the piast of Loch Neagh,
And the monster of Glen-an-smoil.

The Piast of Loch Erne, though a blue one, fell by his hand.
And the furious Piast of Loch Riathach;
He slew—though brave their hearts
A piast and cat at Ath-cliath.

He slew the spectre' of Loch Lein,
Great was the prowess to undertake the attack;
He slew the spectre of Drumcliabh,
The Spectre and Piast of Loch Ree.
Fionn of the noble heart slew.
The spectre of Glen Righe of the highways;
And every piast by the valor of his keen blade,
In the glens of Eire he annihilated.

The Spectre and Piast of Glen-h-Arma (Glenarm),
Though powerful, Fionn slew
Fionn expelled from the Raths,
Every piast he went to meet.

And a piast on the Shannon, a cause of joy.
That disturbed the happiness of men;
He slew by frequenting the deep (lake).
The Piast of Loch Ramar of the conflicts.

He killed—great the destruction
The monster of Sliabh Guillin, though fierce;
And the two Piasts of Glen Inny,
Also fell by his sword.

There was a piast in loch Meilge,
A match in bravery for the hand of Fionn ;
And the huge Piast of Loch Carra,
Together with the monster of Loch Truim.

There was a piast in Loch Masg,
Who kept in terror the men of Fail (Ireland)
He slew it with his victorious sword.
Though the task was great for any individual.

In Loch Laeghaire there always was a piast
That was wont to light fires
Despite all the treacherous means it used.
With his arms he beheaded it.
The monster of Drobhaois, proved in brave acts.
And the idiot of the mountain of Clare;
Fionn slew with Mac-an-Luinn,
Though their conflict and battles were dreadful.

The monster of Loch Lurgan, though active.
By Fionn of the Fenians it fell
It shall not be recorded till the day of doom.
The destruction he dealt upon hosts.

The piast of the murmuring Bann fell.
By the hand of Fionn of the hard conflicts;
Numerous the losses we sustained by their strength.
Until they were destroyed by Fionn.

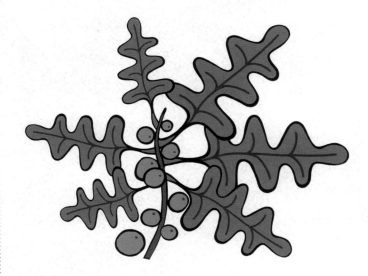

ACKNOWLEDGEMENTS

I would like to thank Michael Brennan, who has been so generous with his time and vast experience. Also Mags Gargan, Alba Esteban, Garry O'Sullivan and all the people at Currach Press, who have made this such an enjoyable project.

Special thanks to my family, Kathleen, Sadie and Alice, who are a constant reminder of the existence of magic.